SOCCER MANIA!

by Erika Tamar
Illustrated by Dee deRosa

A STEPPING STONE BOOK

Random House New York

For Michael,
and special thanks
to the fabulous Bookends
—E. T.

Text copyright © 1993 by Erika Tamar
Illustrations copyright © 1993 by Dee deRosa
All rights reserved under International and Pan-American Copyright Conventions. Published in the United States by Random House, Inc., New York, and simultaneously in Canada by Random House of Canada Limited, Toronto.

Library of Congress Cataloging-in-Publication Data
Tamar, Erika.
  Soccer mania! / by Erika Tamar ; illustrated by Dee deRosa.
  p. cm.
  "A Stepping Stone book."
  Summary: Nine-year-old Pete and his friends, who enjoy playing pick-up soccer, get registered as an official team and discover the negative aspects of competition.
  ISBN 0-679-83396-X (pbk.)—ISBN 0-679-93396-4 (lib. bdg.)
  [1. Soccer—Fiction.] I. deRosa, Dee, ill. II. Title.
PZ7.T159So 1993
[Fic]—dc20   92-37837

Manufactured in the United States of America   10 9 8 7

Contents

•1•
At the
Pleasant Avenue Lot

I couldn't figure out why Mr. Ferris, Mudball's dad, was watching us. Mudball, Tony, Sue, Jonathan, Fred, Larry, and me—I'm Pete—were playing soccer in the vacant lot on Pleasant Avenue that August afternoon. Mr. Ferris stood at the fence with his briefcase at his feet. Why was he staring at every move we made?

"Hey, Pete!" Tony yelled. He kicked the soccer ball to me. Tony was my best friend all through third grade last year. I kicked it back. Then Sue came streaking by and stole the ball.

"Over here, Sue!" called Mudball. He trapped the ball and booted it to Larry. Larry's only a second grader, but he's big for his age. He lives next door to me. I think he got mature from hanging out with us.

I looked over at the fence. Mr. Ferris was still there. He usually just waved to Mudball when he passed by on his way home from work. But yesterday he'd stayed and watched for a long time. And then he showed up today, too. Why would a grownup be hanging around?

"To me!" Jonathan shouted. Then he was dribbling the ball across the lot. All of us chased after him. Fred's sneaker laces were untied again and he ran right out of his shoe. He started laughing and hopping after the ball on one leg. That broke everybody up and we all stopped, except for my dog, Spot. Spot had his nose on the ball, moving it along. It looked so funny.

I looked over at Mr. Ferris. He was frowning.

"Hey, Pete, I want your dog on my side," Tony said.

"He's faster than anybody," Jonathan said.

"Not faster than *me*." That was Sue. She's the best runner because her legs are so long.

"I bet he'd beat you in a race," Jonathan said.

Spot loved soccer. He had so much fun barking and jumping alongside us. He doesn't have any spots. I named him when I was too little to know better.

Tony ran to get the ball. He threw it in the air and jumped for it. He hit it back to us with his forehead. We watched it soar.

"That's using your head," Fred said.

Tony grinned. "I guess I'm a natural. Like the great Pelé."

"Who's Pelé?" I asked.

"The world's greatest athlete, that's all," Tony said. "My brother gave me a book about him. *The Kid from Brazil.* I'll show you."

Tony usually didn't read that much. Jonathan was the one who always had his nose in a book.

We all started bouncing the ball off our heads and shoulders. We were getting pretty good because we played soccer almost every day. Tony's big brother Sal is on the high school soccer team. He'd told us to work on dribbling with our weaker foot. He'd told us to practice juggling the ball off our knees. We more or less got the hang of it. Well, Fred didn't—he was an awkward kid with thick glasses—but he tried hard.

Sometimes other kids from the neighborhood—Charlie, Mike, Dan, and those guys—played with us. If there were enough people, we'd split into teams. Shirts against skins. We used some old wood planks we'd found in Sue's garage for the goals. We never quit until it got too dark to see or we were worn-out tired or our mothers started calling us home for dinner.

"Come on, let's play. Over here, Pete!"

I kicked the ball and it made a good, satisfying *thwunk*. It sailed to Sue. As I ran past the fence, I saw Mr. Ferris take a notebook out of his briefcase. When I checked later, he was writing in it. Frowning. It made me feel funny. Finally he left.

When we stopped to rest, I asked Mudball, "What's your dad doing? Why is he watching us?"

"I don't know."

Tony said, "He called my dad last night."

"He called my house, too," Jonathan said. "There's going to be a big parents' meeting tonight. At your place, Pete."

"What about?" I asked.

Mudball shrugged. "Something about soccer."

Uh-oh. There was a parents' meeting last spring when I chased a high fly baseball through Mrs. Johnson's daffodils. They all kind of flattened out. Her garden is right next to the vacant lot. It was my very best catch ever, but Mrs. Johnson didn't care about that.

"You think we're in trouble again?"

"We didn't do anything," Tony said. He looked worried. "Did we?"

"Sue," I said. "What about those wood planks?" They were pretty old and wormy. What if they were some kind of antiques?

"I told you, my folks don't want them," Sue said. "Anyway, no one called *my* house about any meeting."

"Maybe it's Spot," Fred said. "Maybe his barking bothers Mrs. Johnson."

Spot's heart would break if I had to leave him home. His tail always started wagging the minute he saw the black-and-white ball.

"Nah, it's not Spot," Tony said. "Mrs. Johnson likes dogs. She has two Pekingese."

"Yeah, but they're *pedigreed*," Jonathan said.

"Well, it's at your house, Pete," Tony said. "You better listen in."

I sure would.

•2•
Good News
and Bad News

They were all in our living room. I pressed against the wall outside the doorway. I could hear Mr. Ferris through the clatter of coffee cups.

"Get things organized . . ." he was saying.

I heard forks scraping plates—I hoped they wouldn't eat up all of Mom's chocolate cake—and Mr. Ferris again. "College scholarships . . ." he said. "For the good of the kids . . . If everyone agrees . . ."

College scholarships? I'd just finished third grade!

"Sounds fine to me." That was my dad.

"Excellent sport . . ." Mr. Ruggiero, Tony's dad, was saying. "When I was a boy in Italy . . ."

Then Mr. Ferris's voice started up again. "A lot of talent here . . . Of course, my Arthur will . . ."

I'd almost forgotten that Mudball's real name was Arthur.

"Get organized for the fall season . . ." Mr.

Ferris continued. "Registration and . . . tell the boys tomorrow . . ."

"Order uniforms . . ." someone said.

Wow! They were talking about us becoming a real team!

I woke up early the next morning. I saw Larry outside and told him the good news. He got all

excited and we ran over to Tony's.

Tony was in his front yard with Mudball and Jonathan. They were grinning like they already knew. When I ran up, we all slapped hands.

"Okay! All right! We're a team!"

"My dad's coaching," Mudball said, "and we'll be in the county soccer league and play against other towns and"—Mudball stopped to catch his breath—"we're the Shorehaven Smashers!"

"We are?"

"My dad picked the name. He started doing the paperwork last night."

It would have been fun to pick our own name— but Smashers wasn't bad.

"We could be the Kids from Brazil," Tony said.

"That's nuts. We're from Shorehaven," Jonathan said.

"But in honor of Pelé—"

"Pelé wasn't the world's greatest athlete," Jonathan said. "What about Babe Ruth? Or Muhammad Ali? Or . . ." He was very smart and liked to get everything exact.

"Pelé was too the greatest!" Tony was getting mad.

"In soccer," Jonathan said.

"Well, that's what we're talking about!" Tony said.

"My dad's ordering the uniforms," Mudball said. "Blue and white."

"Uniforms and everything!" Tony said. "I want to be number 10, like Pelé."

"I want to be number 7," Larry said. "For good luck."

"Wait a minute," Mudball said. He scuffed his shoe along the ground. "Uh . . . you can't be on the team, Larry."

We all stared at Mudball.

It took a while before Larry could say, "Why not?"

"We need Larry," I said. "He's good."

"I'm good," Larry repeated.

"I know," Mudball said. "My dad said it was a real shame—but you're too young. We're a nine-year-old team. Everyone has to be nine. It's a rule."

"Larry's big for his age," Jonathan said. "He's bigger than Fred."

"Dad said we have to show birth certificates

for registration and get picture ID's and stuff," Mudball said.

Larry's face turned red. "That's not fair!"

"It's a rule," Mudball repeated. "We're sorry, but—"

Larry looked like he was trying hard not to cry.

"Maybe you can find an eight-year-old team . . ." I said.

Larry glared at me. "I want my Archie comics

back! All of them! Right now! Today!"

"Aw, come on, Larry . . ." I didn't have the heart to ask him for my Spidermans.

Larry turned away fast. "All right for you guys! All right!" We watched him run away down the block.

I felt terrible. "I didn't hear *that* last night."

"Well, don't say anything to Sue. She's not on the team either."

"What are you talking about?" Sue was faster than anybody.

"My dad says no girls on boys' teams," said Mudball.

"But Sue's good!" Tony said. "Almost as good as me."

"My dad says it's a soccer league rule," Mudball mumbled. "Something about—you know—those things on their chests."

"Sue doesn't even have those things yet!" I said.

That was exactly when she came riding over on her bike.

"Hi!" she said cheerfully. "What did you find out about the parents' meeting?"

"Who's gonna tell her?" I said.

"Not me," Tony said.

"Tell me what?"

We all looked at each other. Then everybody looked at Mudball.

He said it very fast. "We're the Shorehaven Smashers in the county soccer league and there're no girls."

"That's dumb," Sue said. "That's about the dumbest thing I ever heard."

"Yeah," Tony said.

"That really stinks," she said.

"Yeah," I agreed.

Mudball shrugged. "It's a county soccer league rule."

There was a pause. "So what are you guys going to do about it?" she said.

I looked down at the ground.

"A dumb rule," Tony said.

Sue bit her lip. "What am I supposed to do now?" There was a long silence. "I guess I'm supposed to play with Laurie and Gwendolyn. They dress and undress Barbie dolls all day long. That's all they do."

I couldn't think of anything worse. "Maybe you could be our cheerleader or—"

She gave me a cold stare.

"Hey, Sue," Tony said, "we'll still kick a ball around in the lot sometimes and—"

"Oh, sure," she said. "Sure we will." She turned her bike around and yelled "Thanks for nothing" over her shoulder. Then she rode off without looking back.

"Sue was really good," Tony said sadly. "Well,

that leaves us and Charlie, Mike, Dan, Fred, and—"

"I don't know about Fred," Mudball said.

"Why? Fred's nine," I said.

"My dad says he's not good enough. He trips on his own feet."

Nobody could argue with that.

"But he's nice," I said. "Everybody likes him."

"He's funny," Jonathan added.

"I know, but . . . My dad says he'll coach us right to number one."

"Number one?" Tony's eyes got big. "Us?"

"There'll be tryouts," Mudball said. "My dad says we'll get the best guys and—"

"Maybe if Fred practices a lot before the tryouts," I said.

"Right," Tony said. "We'll help him."

"My dad says tryouts are next week."

Tony and I looked at each other. We'd better get busy with Fred right away.

•3•
Tryouts

"It's no use," Fred said. "I'm not gonna make it."

We were sitting on the bed in Tony's room. We'd been practicing with Fred all day. Tryouts were going to be that night.

"Don't give up," Tony said. "Maybe if you look at the pictures . . ." He had that book about Pelé, *The Kid from Brazil.* The pages were rumpled and fingerprinted.

"What good's that going to do?" Fred said.

"Look at the way he stands and kicks," Tony said. "Make believe you're Pelé. . . . That's what I do."

At tryouts that night Fred was trying so hard
to look like Pelé that once he missed the ball
completely. I saw Mr. Ferris writing in his notebook.

We were in the junior high gym. There were
kids from the Pleasant Avenue lot and others that

I'd never even seen before. There were more than fifty altogether. I thought it would be just the guys from the neighborhood. Mr. Ferris was going to choose sixteen—eleven players and five subs. What if I wasn't chosen? Tony would get on for sure, but what about me?

Dad was there, and some of the other fathers. Mr. Ferris was in charge.

"Listen up, boys," he said. "You get points for each skill, and numbers don't lie. The highest total scores get on the team. So let's see you do your best."

We had to kick the ball one at a time, aiming for the space between two cones. My mouth felt dry. When my turn came, I knocked a cone over. Would that count as close, or what? Mr. Ferris was writing. Dad looked worried. He was shaking his head. Well, Mudball missed by a mile.

We had to dribble balls across the floor of the gym. Jonathan was good at that. I felt nervous with all the grownups staring. My feet weren't working right. I *had* to make the team!

Then we were supposed to race to the opposite side in groups of five. Ten points for first place,

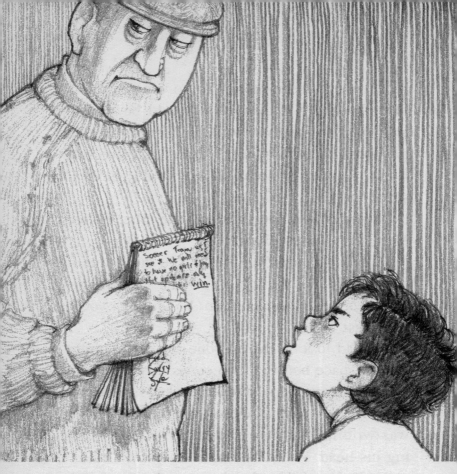

eight points for second, six points for third . . .
I knew I was a fast runner—I'd almost tied with
Sue once.

The other fathers spread out in the gym to score
other groups. Mudball and I were in Mr. Ferris's
group.

"Ready, set, *go!*"

I pushed off as hard as I could. My sneakers were speeding over the floor. All I could hear was the rush of my breath. Halfway there. Almost there. I didn't think about anything else. I kept my eyes on the wall ahead. I touched it first, pounding into it, gasping, just ahead of Mudball!

"Arthur first—ten points. Pete second—eight points. Charlie third . . ." Mr. Ferris was saying.

I couldn't believe it. "I was first, Mr. Ferris!"

"No, Pete," he said. "You were second. That's very good."

"But . . . but . . . Tell him, Mudball!"

Mudball looked at his dad and then down at the floor. He didn't say anything.

"Second place is fine, Pete. Don't worry about it," Mr. Ferris said. He turned away. "Next group, let's go, hurry up!"

I found my dad at the other end of the gym, refereeing another race. "Dad, I came in first and Mr. Ferris said Mudball—Arthur—did!"

Dad looked at me, puzzled. "Maybe it was very close and you thought—"

"No, I came in first!"

"Pete, it must be a mistake. Mr. Ferris wouldn't do that."

But he did do that.

When tryouts were over, my friends met in the hallway. I didn't say anything about the race. I'd sound like a sore loser.

"Did anybody kick through the cones?" I asked.

"No," Jonathan said. "I came close, though."

"I did," Tony said, "right straight through." Tony made the thumbs-up sign. "And I was first in dribbling."

Everyone knew Tony was the best. "You'll be on the team for sure," I said.

"We all better be," Tony said. "I don't want to be with a bunch of kids I don't know."

Fred didn't stop to talk to us. I saw him go out the door fast, head down. I felt bad for Fred, but right then I was worried about myself.

"When are we going to find out?" I asked.

"The fathers are adding up the scores tonight. They'll let us know," Jonathan said. "Tomorrow morning."

What if all my friends got on the team and I didn't? What would I do for the rest of my life?

•4•
Practice Makes Perfect

I watched Dad sleeping. Every once in a while he let out a breath with a little whistle. Mom was curled up with her arm over her face. They'd kill me if I woke them this early—but I'd die if I didn't find out right away.

I stared at Dad's closed eyes. "Open," I mouthed silently. "Open. Now."

He sighed and burrowed into the pillow.

At this rate he could sleep for another hour!

"Dad?" I said. And then louder, "Dad!"

He bolted upright. "What? What? What time is it?"

"Dad, did I make the team? Did I?"

He snuggled back under the covers and put the pillow over his head. "Mmmm."

"Does that mean yes?"

"Mmmm-hmmm," he mumbled.

"I did? I made it? I made it!"

"Six o'clock in the morning." Mom's voice was foggy. "Go back to sleep, Pete."

I found out more over pancakes at breakfast. Me, Tony, Jonathan, Mudball, Mike, Charlie, and Dan were on the team!

"There'll be practice every evening," Dad was saying. "School starts Monday—"

I groaned.

"And you'll have to get all your homework done in the afternoon. I want your promise."

"I will, Dad. I promise." I'd do anything!

Mom was stirring the pitcher of orange juice. "With games every weekend you won't have much time for anything else."

Me, a Shorehaven Smasher! Pancakes, oozing blueberries, were my favorite things in the whole world. I swallowed a big mouthful.

"Mr. Ferris is planning a heavy schedule," Dad

said. "The syrup, please. It sounds a little ambitious, but—"

"Does Mr. Ferris have to be the coach?"

"Well, he volunteered and—"

"When do we get our uniforms? When does practice start?" I couldn't wait!

The first practice was at the junior high. We had the field from six o'clock until dark. The grass was nice and smooth, with no weeds or rocks to stop the ball, and there were real goals. It was much better than the vacant lot. The bad part was that Spot couldn't come. He whimpered at the door when I left without him.

We started with warm-ups—sprints around the track and stretches and sit-ups. We had to do a *lot* of sit-ups. Halfway through, I collapsed on the grass.

We worked on skills. We learned to kick with the inside of our feet for better control. We practiced trapping the ball. We formed two long lines and worked on passing. While we were waiting in line for our turns, Jonathan and I started wrestling a little just to pass the time.

"Jonathan! Pete!" Mr. Ferris called. "No horsing around." And a little while later, when Mudball was talking to Tony, "Cut it out, Arthur."

It was hard to wait in line without doing anything. Mr. Ferris wanted us to pay attention all the time. "Listen up, men. You can learn from watching the others."

I liked the way he said "Listen up, men." He treated us like pros. He said we didn't have to call him Mr. Ferris, "Coach" would be okay. And when I trapped the ball just right, he said "Way to go, Pete!" and patted my shoulder.

We took turns kicking at the goal. Big redheaded Dan was our goalie. Mr. Ferris wanted to give him lots of practice. Dan made some great saves at first, but when we kept on booting the ball at him, he started losing it.

"I'm getting tired, Coach," he said.

Mr. Ferris frowned. "Athletes don't fold under pressure." He looked around at everyone. "Who's going to be number one?"

"Shorehaven Smashers!" we all yelled as we kept bombarding the goal.

After a while, it got boring to do the same things

over and over. It wasn't much like playing.

Mudball wasn't that good and his dad shook his head in disappointment. "Arthur, stop dreaming! Kick it in, Arthur! Try again, champ."

Mudball flushed.

Mr. Ferris kept us working until dark.

"Maybe we could get some lights here," he muttered.

I was glad we didn't have lights. By the time we walked home, my feet were dragging.

"I thought this was supposed to be fun," Jonathan said.

"Feels a lot like school," I said.

"We're learning a lot of good stuff, though," Tony said. "And athletes have to work hard, right?"

"Right."

"My dad says—"

Lately, everything out of Mudball's mouth started with "My dad says."

"—we need to be ready for the game on Saturday."

We all perked up at that. A real game coming up, with uniforms and everything!

• 5 •
The North Bay Maniacs

I passed the vacant lot on my way home from school. Sue and Fred were there, kicking an old soup can around.

Fred looked glad to see me. "Hey, Pete!"

"Hi." I stopped and shifted my schoolbooks to my other arm. I'd missed him.

"You want to play kick the can?"

"Uh, I can't. I have to do my homework."

"*Now?*"

"Well, see, I have to get it all done before dinner because then there's practice and—"

"How's practice?" Sue said.

It had been every single night that week. "It's not that great," I said.

Sue looked like she didn't believe me. "Uh-huh," she said.

"I never even get to watch *Mutant Mice from Mars* anymore," I said. Homework before dinner, and I had to eat early, all by myself, because otherwise the food bounced around in my stomach.

"There's nothing to do around here anymore," Sue said.

Sometimes I used to like doing nothing.

"How about tomorrow?" Fred said. "Let's play navy down by the stream and—"

"Tomorrow's Saturday," I said. "Our first game. We're going over to North Bay and I don't know when we'll be back."

"You guys are so lucky," Sue said.

On Saturday morning we were the first to arrive at the North Bay field. We drove up in a big caravan of cars because all the parents wanted to come, too. Even Mom. Mom was never interested in seeing baseball or hockey on TV with me and Dad. She said she liked to *do* sports, not *watch* them. Mom plays a lot of tennis.

But now she was beaming. "This will be fun."

"I thought you didn't like to watch sports," I said.

"It's different when your son is on the team," Mom said. "I'm a true-blue Smashers fan!"

We piled out of the cars and ran onto the field. Our brand-new uniforms sparkled in the sunshine. They were neat. We had blue shorts and white T-shirts with SHOREHAVEN SMASHERS in blue letters on the front and our last names and numbers on the back. The T-shirt sizes got mixed up, so Tony's was tight and Jonathan's hung to his knees, but that was all right. We looked sharp. And we had brand-new shin guards under our tube socks and brand-new soccer cleats. We started warm-ups with a lot of spirit. All the parents seemed excited, too.

And then the North Bay Maniacs came onto the scene.

They were wearing black-and-purple-striped shirts—real shirts with collars and long sleeves. They did their sit-ups with no sweat at all, counting out loud. When they stood up, they

flexed their muscles and snarled at us. They looked like they ate razor blades with their Wheaties in the morning.

Both teams lined up while the coaches showed the referee our picture ID's and birth certificates.

The referee checked our feet for illegal football
cleats. He sure didn't trust anybody. Then both
teams went into huddles.

"North Bay Maniacs!" we heard them yelling.
"Number one!"

"Listen up, men," Mr. Ferris said, and the parents crowded around, too. "Pete, Jonathan, Richie, Kevin on defense. Remember, play your positions. Arthur, center forward. Tony, left forward, and Mike, right forward. Pass to Arthur, and Arthur, you kick it in."

Tony looked surprised. "But Mr. Ferris—"

Mudball looked nervous. "But Dad, Tony can—"

"Pass to Arthur," Mr. Ferris said. "Set it up for the goal." He looked down at Mudball. "Think like a winner, son!"

Mr. Ruggiero, Tony's dad, started muttering a whole stream of Italian that no one could understand.

"All right," Mr. Ferris said. "Who's number one?"

"Shorehaven Smashers!" we yelled as we trotted onto the field.

The Maniacs won the face-off, and the ball came speeding to our end. I tried to stop one of their forwards, but he plowed right through me. I got a sharp elbow in the ribs and the pattern of his cleats on my thigh.

"Kill that kid!" yelled the Maniacs' parents.

Jonathan got the ball away and booted it forward. Tony got it next.

"Go, Tony! Go, Tony!" our parents were screaming. I saw Mom out of the corner of my eye, and she was kicking and kicking at the grass like she was in the game herself.

Tony passed to Mudball, and he went for the goal and missed. Mr. Ruggiero was screaming in Italian and Mr. Ferris was screaming in English.

The ball went up and down the field.

"Pete, stay back!" Mr. Ferris shouted. "Stay back!"

"Go with the flow, Pete!" my dad shouted.

"Kick it! Kick it *hard*!" Mr. Ferris yelled. "Get it in, Arthur!"

The sun was in my eyes and I was getting a headache. We kept setting it up for Mudball and Mudball kept losing it and looking like he wanted to cry.

"A goal, Arthur!" Mr. Ferris's voice was loud and clear above the rest. "A goal!"

One of the Maniacs smashed past me.

"Stop him, Pete!"

"Go, Maniacs!"

The Maniac booted the ball into our goal and Dan couldn't block it. There was a roar from the Maniacs' side. I was afraid to look at Mr. Ferris.

When we came off the field after the first half, the Maniacs were winning two to nothing. Jonathan's mom was passing out orange sections and water, and Mr. Ferris was jumping up and down.

"You played like a bunch of girls out there! A bunch of girls!" he screamed.

We sure could have used Sue on our team.

"What's the matter with you?" Mr. Ferris snarled at Mudball. "You looked like a loser out there!"

Mudball's voice started shaking. "But Dad, I couldn't—"

"What kind of a Ferris are you, anyway?"

Mudball's face got all red. "It's Dan's fault," he said. "We need a good goalie."

Dan's lips were trembling. "It's not *my* fault."

Mudball pointed at him. "You let them get two goals."

"Wait a minute!" Dan's dad got into it. "That

ball passed through ten of you guys before it ever got to the goal!"

Then Mr. Ruggiero told Mr. Ferris to put Tony in center forward where he belonged and Mr. Ferris started screaming in this high, strange voice and Mr. Ruggiero was waving both his hands in the air. The grownups were crowding around and pointing at each other and trying to keep Mr. Ruggiero and Mr. Ferris apart.

Across the field the Maniacs looked happy. Maybe their coach had just thrown them some raw meat.

•6•
The Second Half

Mr. Ferris and Mr. Ruggiero were still nose to nose, shouting at each other, as I finished up my last orange section. Charlie's mother tugged at Mr. Ferris's sleeve.

"Excuse me."

She tugged hard until they both stopped and stared at her.

"Can you put Charlie in for the second half?" she asked.

"I'll see. I don't know," Mr. Ferris mumbled.

"But Charlie hasn't—"

I looked over at Charlie. His uniform was the only one that was still totally clean. He hadn't even made it onto the field yet.

"Competitive situation . . ." Mr. Ferris muttered. "Not quite ready . . . maybe later . . ." Mr. Ferris pulled his arm out of Charlie's mother's reach while Mr. Ruggiero kept on screaming in his face. I think Mr. Ferris was about to punch him, but Charlie's mom got in the way and was doing some screaming of her own.

Then it was time to get into a huddle. "Listen up, men. We're going to be winners. Winners! Winners!" Mr. Ferris's eyes had a strange gleam. "You're going to score, Arthur. Understand me, Arthur? Score! Dan, shape up! Winners! Kick the ball hard. Kick it *hard*!"

"Yes, Coach," we said.

"Who's number one?"

"Smashers," we said weakly as we staggered back onto the field.

"Smashers!" our parents yelled. I could hear my dad's voice loud and clear above the rest.

The second half didn't start out much better than the first. The Maniacs booted the ball toward our side. I ran for it. I didn't notice that Jonathan was going for it too. We collided and knocked each other down. Dan made a great save.

"Morons! Idiots!" Mr. Ferris pulled Jonathan and me out of the game. Everyone was staring at us. Mr. Ferris was hopping mad. "What have I been telling you? Play your positions!" He sent two other guys in. Not Charlie.

I hadn't *meant* to run into Jonathan. I'd been doing my best. What if I made another mistake? Mr. Ferris would yell at me again. That's if he even let me play again.

I watched from the side. One of the Maniacs ran into Tony and knocked the wind out of him. Tony had to lie down to get back his breath. The Maniacs' parents cheered! It was scary, but Tony was okay in a minute and back in the game.

"Kick it! Kick it *hard*!" Mr. Ferris kept shouting. And "Pass to Arthur! Go, champ!"

Mudball had his teeth clenched. He was all over the place, high-kicking and punching Maniacs in the back when the referee wasn't looking. I'd never seen him act like that before.

The ball went up and down the field. Mr. Ferris ran up and down the sidelines, following. Charlie trailed after him in his spotless uniform, looking hopeful.

The referee called Kevin offside. "Turkey," Mr.

Ferris muttered. He pulled Kevin out and sent me in.

A Maniac halfback had the ball and started to pass it to a forward. I ran to get between them and I trapped it.

"Center it, Pete!" my dad yelled.

"Up the side!" Mr. Ferris yelled.

Center? Side? A Maniac was coming at me.

"Over here, Pete!" Tony yelled. That was the only voice that made sense to me. I kicked to Tony, and instead of passing to Mudball, Tony dribbled the ball along the side. A bunch of Maniacs were after him, but he faked them out. It was beautiful to see. Tony got a breakaway! He dribbled up the field and kicked, and their goalie fumbled. Our first goal!

The parents went wild and we all gave Tony high-fives.

Then the referee caught a Maniac tripping a Smasher and we got a penalty shot. Mike got into position for it. The Maniacs shouted at their goalie to make the save of a lifetime.

"Block it, Joe! Block it, Joe! Block it, Joe!" they chanted.

The pressure was on. The goalie's eyes were twitching. I almost felt sorry for him. He didn't have a chance against a direct kick. The kick came.

Mike scored and we were tied!

Mr. Ferris was a wild man, and the other parents lost it, too. "One more! One more! Do it, Smashers!" The ball skittered back and forth, and the Maniac and Smasher parents were trying to outshout each other. And finally, just before time was up, Tony did it again! That was terrific, considering that two of the Maniacs were trying to murder him at the time. We won by one goal. We jumped into a big happy pile around Tony. The grownups were so overjoyed you'd think they'd placed million-dollar bets on the game.

Then both teams had to line up to shake hands. I could hear the mothers saying, "Isn't that cute?" and "Don't you love that part?"

I went through the line and my hand was getting all this wet, sticky stuff on it. The Maniacs were spitting on their hands just before they offered them to us! I memorized their faces. If we ever played them again, I'd kick every one of them in the shins.

As we came off the field Mr. Ferris patted our heads and said, "Good work, men."

Mom was running around saying to everyone, "My son got the assist! My son! The assist!" It was very embarrassing.

Mr. Ferris was all smiles. "Drop the boys off at Gino's," he said to the other parents. "Pizza for lunch. My treat."

Winning was great!

•7•
Shape Up or Ship Out

At Gino's we pulled three tables together for the sixteen of us and Mr. Ferris. I like pizza more than anything, especially the way they make it at Gino's, with thick crust and pepperoni and cheese dripping all over the place, but I was almost too excited to eat. Everyone was feeling good and yelling from one end of the tables to the other.

"Did you see that save in the second half?" There was tomato sauce running down Dan's chin. "Didn't think I'd make it."

"It was awesome!"

"That big Maniac, number 8, was the worst," Jonathan said.

"Yeah, he was practicing karate kicks on me."

We were all chiming in, rehashing the game. Except for Charlie. He didn't have much to say.

"How about that breakaway?" Tony said.

"That was really something!"

"Just a minute, Tony. You have nothing to be proud of," Mr. Ferris said. "You were supposed to pass to Arthur."

Tony looked startled.

"I'm not saying it wasn't a good goal," Mr. Ferris said, "but you didn't follow instructions. You have to learn to do what you're told."

Tony had that look he gets when he's mad and trying to hold it in.

"And that goes for all of you. Pete, I told you to kick it up the side, didn't I? Passing to Tony was a stupid move."

"But we got the goal," I said.

"Dumb luck."

Suddenly it became very quiet at Gino's.

"If the Maniac defense knew what it was doing . . . Look, there's *strategy* involved in this game. Pass those napkins, Mike." Mr. Ferris took a pen out of his shirt pocket and started scrib-

bling on the napkins. "Gather around, boys, and watch." He kept talking and drawing lots of arrows in different directions. I couldn't make head or tail of them and I don't think anyone else could either.

"Next week we meet the Lakeview Bone-Crushers. That's the team to beat, and you need a *lot* of practice. I don't think I can get a field for this afternoon—"

"This afternoon?" everyone wailed.

"—but definitely tomorrow. Double practice tomorrow."

"Uh, Mr. Ferris, that's Sunday, and I have to—" Kevin started.

"No excuses," Mr. Ferris said.

"I have to go to my friend's birthday party."

"No excuses! You don't show for practice, you're off the team. Is that perfectly clear?"

"But Mr. Ferris," Jonathan said, "my grandmother expects me to—"

"Listen up. One lucky win doesn't make you pros. Tomorrow we're going over your mistakes"—he glared at Jonathan and me—"and you made plenty of mistakes. So shape up or ship out."

The pizza formed lumps in my stomach.

"Now watch this," Mr. Ferris said. One of the arrows doubled back in a squiggly circle. "The way to spearhead an attack . . ."

Mr. Ferris went on and on. I stopped listening after a while. I was thinking.

When we left Gino's, we stood in a group on the sidewalk outside.

"Tomorrow," he said. "At the junior high. Eleven *sharp*."

"But Mr. Ferris," Jonathan said again.

Mr. Ferris wasn't listening. His eyes were glazed over. "I'll turn the Smashers into a winning machine!" he growled. "We'll chew up those Bone-Crushers and spit 'em out!"

I just wanted to be a kid playing ball.

•8•
The Pleasant Avenue Lot

On Sunday morning I woke up with a hollow feeling. It felt like the morning I had to go to school and there was going to be a test on a chapter I'd forgotten to read. I wasn't looking forward to practice.

I thought I'd take Spot for a walk first. Poor Spot. I hadn't had much time for him ever since the Smashers started.

It was a nice day and Spot was happy to be out sniffing at everything. I didn't want to take him right back home. It was still early. I threw a stick and he went after it. Then we ran down the street together, all the way to the fence at the

end of Pleasant Avenue. Fred and Sue and some of the kids I'd seen at tryouts were playing in the vacant lot. Larry was there, too.

Spot wagged his tail the minute he saw that black-and-white ball, and before I could stop him, he was in the lot and running after it.

I heard Fred say, "Hi, Spot. How're you doing, buddy?" Then he looked toward me.

I waved. He waved back and kept on playing. I watched for a while. It looked like fun.

"To me!" Fred shouted. "Pass to me!"

"Fred, your sneakers are untied again!" Sue called impatiently.

"Time out."

"Okay, okay."

Sue and Fred and some of the other kids came over to the fence. They flopped down on the grass.

"Can't you double-knot them?" Sue said. "Oh, hi, Pete."

"Hi."

"I *do* double-knot them. They get loose."

"Then triple-knot them!" Sue's ponytail swished as she turned to me. "So how was your game?"

"We won."

"Well, that's good." She didn't seem too interested.

"Come on, guys." Larry stood up. "Let's play!"

"All right, I'm ready," Fred said. He started to follow the others and then hesitated. "You want to play, Pete?"

"I can't . . . I have to . . . uh . . . Well, just for a little while." It couldn't be eleven yet.

"It's shirts against skins," Sue said. "Who wants Pete?"

"I guess we'll take Pete," Larry said. "They're winning, three to two."

I took off my T-shirt and added it to the pile against the fence.

"Isn't that Tony over there?" Fred said.

We watched him walking down the sidewalk toward us.

"We'll take Tony!" Sue said. "Hurry up, Tony, come on!"

Tony came running and the next thing I knew, I was dribbling and Sue stole the ball from me and laughed the way she always did, and then Tony kicked for a goal and I got ready for the face-off and . . .

"Wait. Hold it. We've got to go to practice," Tony said. "Pete? It's five to eleven."

"It is?"

"We can make it to the junior high in time," he said. "If we run."

"Yeah, but . . . I have to take Spot home first."

"I'll take him home for you," Fred said.

"Thanks. Okay, but—"

"But what?" Tony said.

"Yeah, we'd better go or we'll be in bad trouble."

"We'll be off the team," Tony said.

We looked at each other.

"You better get moving then," Sue said.

We just stood there.

"What's the matter with you guys? Don't you like the soccer league?"

"It's weird," I said.

Tony shook his head. "You wouldn't believe how weird."

"We can make it if we run," I said.

"If we start running right now."

"Mr. Ferris will be mad if we're late."

"I bet he'll yell blue murder at us," Tony said.

I didn't want to get yelled at again. "We better run *fast*!"

"I guess so."

Somehow I couldn't make my feet move. "You go ahead, Tony." I took a deep breath. Making big decisions was tough. Mom and Dad had such a great time at the game. I knew they'd be disappointed. "I'm not going. I'm having more fun here."

"Me too."

"But Tony, you're a *natural*. You ought to be on a real team."

"I know. My brother Sal says the junior high and high school teams are good. Anyway, even Pelé didn't turn pro until he was in his teens. He played lots of soccer with his friends on the streets of Brazil, just fooling around and having fun. It's in the book. I'll show you."

"Wow," Larry said. "And you had uniforms, and everything."

I forgot about that! Mom and Dad had just bought me a brand-new uniform and cleats. They might get real mad.

"Maybe we better go," I said. I put on my shirt.

"Not me. I'm not going."

"How will your dad take it?" I asked Tony.

"He doesn't like Mr. Ferris that much. Did you know my dad was on a championship team in Italy? Last night he said maybe he ought to start a new team for me and my friends and coach it himself."

"Oh?"

"I told him no thanks. Anyway, my mom said no, he gets too excited."

"Well, are you guys going or staying or what?" Sue said.

I was thinking Mom and Dad had pretty much liked me for nine years before I ever became a Smasher. And I could still wear the cleats at the Pleasant Avenue lot. I'd tell Mom they'd still be useful.

"Staying," I said.

"Staying," Tony said. He grinned. "Mr. Ferris will have a fit."

"So what are we waiting for? Let's play soccer!"

We were back in the game and Spot was yipping and running alongside. The sun was shin-

ing and Fred ran right out of his shoe and we couldn't stop laughing. One of the guys passed to Larry. Larry passed to me and I kicked the ball just right with a real nice satisfying *thwack* and man, it went flying!

About the Author

"When my son was seven, he joined a pilot soccer program," says ERIKA TAMAR. "It quickly went from low-key to high-strung. I couldn't believe how competitive it became. There was so much pressure to win, win, win! *Soccer Mania!* is based on his experience." Erika Tamar is the highly acclaimed author of many books for children and young adults. She lives in New York City.

About the Illustrator

DEE DE ROSA loves sports—especially scuba diving, skiing, and horseback riding. But she doesn't like competition when it gets out of hand. "I was glad to get a chance to illustrate *Soccer Mania!*" she says, "because so many kids will identify with its important message about competition." Dee deRosa is the talented illustrator of more than three dozen books. She lives with her husband in Syracuse, New York.